BOOKS
ARE VERY
OOH LA LA!

Maisie Moe

CAMPING IS NOT VERY OOH LA LA!

Maisie Moe

CAMPING IS NOT VERY OOH LA LA!

Poppy Harper

Illustrated by Clare Elsom

LITTLE, BROWN BOOKS FOR YOUNG READERS
www.lbkids.co.uk

With special thanks to Dan Metcalf

LITTLE, BROWN BOOKS FOR YOUNG READERS

First published in Great Britain in 2014 by Little, Brown Books for Young Readers

A CIP catalogue record for this book
is available from the British Library.

ISBN 978-0-349-00155-5

Typeset in Humanist by M Rules
Printed and bound in Great Britain by
Clays Ltd, St Ives plc

Papers used by LBYR are from well-managed forests
and other responsible sources.

MIX
Paper from
responsible sources
FSC
www.fsc.org FSC® C104740

Little, Brown Books for Young Readers
An imprint of
Little, Brown Book Group
100 Victoria Embankment
London EC4Y 0DY

An Hachette UK Company
www.hachette.co.uk

www.lbkids.co.uk

To Emmie and Eliza French

My crazy family →

Dad →

Josh, my music mad oldest brother →

Mum with Arthur Stanley, my youngest and most dribbly brother. (only just) →

Me! Maisie Mae. ♡ →

Jack → Football mad and ALWAYS muddy. Gross.

The twins, Harry and Ollie. Don't even ASK. →

CHAPTER ONE

"Attention All Sprogs!"

"Summer is the absolute **BEST**!" said Maisie Mae, placing a family of moles in Bethany's Day-Glo pink palace. "Weeks and weeks of doing whatever we want!"

Maisie Mae was surrounded by toys. She was a having an **EPIC** play date with Bethany-next-door, and they had mixed up all their best-ever toys to make a Sylvanian-Family-Barbie-Bratz super village across her bedroom floor.

It had everything: a playhouse, mansion, shopping mall, schoolhouse, hairdresser's and even a main street with *loads* of shops on.

"I *know*!" said Bethany-next-door, cramming one of Maisie's Barbie dolls into a Sylvanian Family Campervan. "We

can do all the things we can't normally do when we're at school, like . . . like . . ." Bethany stopped as she tried to think of something.

"Practice our 'Boys are stupid' cheerleading dance?" suggested Maisie Mae. "Stay up past our bedtime and watch funny kitten videos on the internet?"

"**EXACTLY**!" said Bethany-next-door.

Maisie Mae smiled. Having Bethany-next-door as a best friend was **COMPLETELY** brilliant. They were exactly alike in every way. Well, except that Bethany had blonde, straight hair and Maisie's was all curly and brown. And that Maisie had five stinky brothers and Bethany didn't have any. Apart from that, they were *completely* the same, which is why it was going to be extra-horrible when Bethany-next-door went on holiday.

"Did you know it's only one week, six days, four hours and three minutes until Mum and Dad whisk me away to Florida?" asked Bethany dreamily.

"Yes," sighed Maisie Mae. "You said. I'm going to miss you loads and loads and loads!"

"Aw, I'll miss you too Maisie Mae!" said Bethany-next-door. She gave her friend a hug. "No, you won't! You'll be too busy having fun at Disney World and making friends with ultra-cool Americans!" laughed Maisie. She gasped. "Maybe you'll meet a real-life film star! They have loads in America!"

"**ATTENTION ALL SPROGS! FAMILY MEETING! KITCHEN! NOW**!" came a bellowing call from downstairs.

"Yikes!" said Maisie Mae, jumping at the sound. "We'd better see what this is all about. Family meetings are always mega-important." She went to the door.

"What about me?" said Bethany-next-door. "I'm not a sprog!"

"Don't worry!" said Maisie Mae. "There are so many of us that Mum and Dad won't even notice. And anyway, you're my best-friend-who-is-almost-as-good-as-a-sister! You *have* to come!"

Maisie Mae pulled her best friend up

from the floor and flung open the door. She stepped into the hall and closed the door behind her, smoothing down the **NO BOYS ALLOWED** sign on the front.

Suddenly there was a **THUMP THUMP THUMP** from the attic bedrooms above. It sounded like a herd of giant centipedes with boots on. Bethany-next-door was about to go down the stairs, but Maisie Mae pulled her back, flattening them both against the wall. It was just as well that she did, or Bethany might have been trampled in the stampede.

Two of Maisie Mae's stinky older brothers came racing down from the second floor. Josh, the eldest, was the first, tapping a rhythm on the walls with a pair of drumsticks as he went. He wore a T-shirt with his favourite band on the front, and his hair was flopping over his eyes as usual.

"Gangway!" he yelled as he passed. "Coming through!"

He was followed by a football bouncing down the stairs, and Jack, the second eldest, clattering down after it. He trapped it as it reached the landing, flipped it up and caught it on the back of his neck.

"Skillzzz!" he said as he passed, spinning the ball on the end of his finger.

Bethany-next-door was about to walk off again when Maisie Mae pulled her back.

"Wait!" she said. "The worst has yet to come!"

The two girls froze as they heard four feet clomping down the stairs. Harry and Ollie, the terrible twins, marched down the landing like soldiers and barged past Maisie and Bethany.

"Hup, two, three, four! Hup, two, three, four!" barked Harry, with Oliver

following behind. The
coast was finally clear,
so the girls stepped out
on to the landing.

"Halt! About turn!"
said Ollie, spinning around.
"Enemy sighted! Fire at will!"

♥ 9 ♥

The girls screamed and ducked as the twins pulled out two water pistols and opened fire on them.

"Aaaargh!" screamed Maisie Mae. "I'll get you two!"

"Oh yeah? How?" said Harry.

"I'll tell Mum!" she said with a smug smile. The twins' faces dropped.

"Not if we get there first!" said Oliver. "Scramble!"

The twins raced down the stairs into the kitchen, followed by Maisie and Bethany.

"Whatever Maisie Mae says, she's fibbing!" said Oliver, out of breath.

"Never mind that! Just sit down and listen to your dad. We've got a **BIG ANNOUNCEMENT**!" said Mum, grabbing the guns from them and storing them in a high cupboard.

Arthur Stanley giggled as Mum swung him around on her hip.

Arthur Stanley was Maisie Mae's only *little* brother, but even though he was small, he made up for it in stinkiness.

"Hi, Mum! Hey, Lil' Bro!" sang Maisie as she passed.

Arthur Stanley gurgled happily, then went cross-eyed as he squeezed out an extra-smelly trump.

Once everyone was sat at the kitchen table, and Arthur Stanley was dribbling happily in his high chair, Mum opened the double doors to the lounge with a flourish.

"Taa-daaaaa!"

Dad stood in the front

room with a flat, round hat on his head and a curly black moustache painted on his face. He was waving a large

blue, white and red flag and a plate full of curly croissants. Everyone stopped talking at once and stared at him.

"I 'ave something very important to tell you!" he announced.

"Why are you talking in that funny voice?" said Jack.

"You will

soon find out, *Jacques*! 'Ere we 'ave the flag of a very famous country. Can you guess which one?"

The boys all started to shout out at once.

"Ireland!" called Josh.

"Egypt!" shouted Oliver.

"Narnia!" said Harry.

"Queens Park Rangers!" yelled Jack.

"What? That's not a . . . Oh, never mind," said Dad, rolling his eyes.

"It's obviously Ireland!" said Josh. "Why else would Dad be putting on that accent?"

The boys started to squabble and the room was soon drowned in the hubbub. Mum went to stand next to Dad. "I don't think they want to hear our big news!" she bellowed at him.

"Yes we do!" Ollie shouted.

"Who wants to hear the big news?" Mum teased.

Maisie Mae put her hand in the air.

"Me! Me!"

"Do you really want to hear it?"

"Yes!" said Jack.

"Really?" said Mum.

"Get on with it!" yelled Josh.

"**OK**!" shouted Dad finally. "The big news is: **WE'RE GOING TO FRANCE ON HOLIDAY**!"

CHAPTER TWO

French Lessons

The kitchen erupted with cheers.

"We're going to France! We're going to France!" sang Maisie Mae and her brothers. They all joined hands and danced around the kitchen table. Arthur Stanley even seemed to join in the song, burping in time to the beat. Maisie Mae broke away and ran up to hug Dad.

"When are we going? Is it soon? Are

we going to fly there? Can Bethany come?" she said, jumping up and down with excitement.

"Sorry, sweetheart," said Mum, detangling her hair from Arthur Stanley's fist. "We'll be going at the same time that Bethany goes on holiday to America."

"In one week, six days, three hours and fifty-three minutes," said Bethany-next-door.

"Um . . . yes, I suppose it is. Unfortunately, it means she won't be able to come," said Dad.

"But . . . but . . . but that means . . ." said Maisie Mae, her eyes widening at the thought. "I'll have to go on holiday with five stinky BOYS, and no girls for a *week!*

"But you'll be in France, having **SO** much fun!" Bethany-next-door said

comfortingly. "I'm *completely* jealous!"
She turned to Mum and Dad and smiled.
"*J'espère que vous apprécierez votre
vacances!*"

Maisie stared open-mouthed at her friend.

"Are you all right, Bethany? You're not making any sense," she said.

"I'm speaking French!" laughed Bethany-next-door. "I said 'I hope you enjoy your holiday'."

"Very impressive!" said Dad.

"*Merci!*" said Bethany with a curtsy.

"Perhaps you could teach Maisie Mae some basic words?" said Mum. "Boys! Those are croissants, not boomerangs!"

"Ooooh, yes!" said Maisie Mae. "You'll have to teach me the very bestest girliest words!"

"And I know just the one to start with!" said Bethany-next-door. "*Rose!*"

"*Rose*," repeated Maisie. "What does it mean?"

"**PINK**!" Bethany burst out laughing.

The two girls giggled as they pranced around the room, saying *rose* in their best French accents.

"Teach me the important words!" said Maisie Mae. "What's 'chocolate'?"

"That's easy. *Chocolat*."

"Cool!" said Josh. "What's 'guitar'?"

"*Guitare*," said Bethany-next-door.

"That's **WELL** easy!" said Jack. "What's 'football'?"

"*Le football!*"

"This is great!" Josh exclaimed. "Most of the words are exactly the same as in

English. You just have to say them like you've got a mouthful of toothpaste!"

They all took turns saying words in a French accent.

"Ah would like le sausage et cheeps," practiced Harry.

"Wiv le sauce de la tomato!" said Oliver.

"Oh, it's going to be beautiful!" said Maisie Mae, pirouetting around the kitchen like a ballerina. "France is so . . . well, *French*! It's glamorous and elegant and *chic*. I'll fit in **PERFECTLY**! There'll be croissants and berets, and poodles and—"

"French fries!" said Harry and Ollie. They turned to Mum and Dad. "Can we go to Disneyland Paris?"

"Yeah!" said Josh. "And climb the Eiffel Tower?"

"And watch Paris St Germain play football?" said Jack.

Mum gave them all a look which silenced them in a second.

How does she do that? thought Maisie Mae.

"We won't be going near any of those things, I'm afraid, folks," she said.

The family groaned. "We'll do a bit of sightseeing, but don't get too excited. We're going to meet up with Auntie Flo and Uncle Jean-Paul at a campsite."

Josh's face dropped.

"*Camping?* As in, tents? Mud? Portaloos?"

"Well, yes. We *will* be in France, but I suppose it'll be just like camping at home," said Dad.

As the kitchen erupted into chaos again, Maisie Mae took Bethany-next-door by the arm and led her back upstairs.

"Are you excited?" said Bethany.

"Of course! Even though we're going camping in the mud, and even though I'll probably have to share a tent with some smelly boys, and even though I'll be away from my best-friend-who-is-almost-as-good-as-a-sister," said Maisie Mae, "I'll be in the most exciting, chic, beautiful country in the world! France is so **OOH LA LA**!"

CHAPTER THREE

Setting Off

Maisie Mae was **DETERMINED** to love every minute of her time in France, but first she had to get there. It was one week, six days, three hours and fifty-three minutes since Dad and Mum had announced they were going on holiday, and Maisie Mae was **TOTALLY** prepared. She had packed her suitcase with loads of sunglasses and sun cream, and learnt lots of must-have

French phrases from Bethany-next-door, including "How much is the chocolate?", "Where is the toilet, please?" and "Please ignore my brothers".

Their car was actually more like a minibus. Before they could drive off, Mum sat everyone in their seats and crammed the luggage in around them.

"Mum, how long will it take to— Ow!" said Maisie, as Mum jabbed a tent under her feet.

"Sorry, sweetie!" said Mum. "Here, just rest this on your lap . . ." She piled a big bag filled with towels on top of her as Harry and Ollie climbed into the seats either side of Maisie Mae. "OK boys, hold these . . ."

Soon, the whole family was squished into the nine seats. In the front sat Mum and Dad, with Arthur Stanley in his special car seat. In the middle, Maisie sat wedged in between Harry and Ollie, and in the back were Josh and Jack. Piled on top of the van and shoved into every spare corner were suitcases, tents, gas stoves and food. The car was jam-packed!

"Mum, I don't think we're going to have room to breathe!" complained Harry as she pushed a picnic chair under his feet and a wash bag on to his lap. Harry and Ollie even had to hold everything in to get the slidey door shut. Maisie Mae was sure that when they got

out, the whole family and their luggage
would spill on to the pavement like
clowns out of a circus car.

Just as they were about to move off,
Maisie heard a muffled groan to the side.

"Er . . . I think I need a wee!" said Ollie
from behind his mountain of bags.

After a quick visit to the toilet and
some frantic re-packing, they drove away.
Jack and Josh had their feet on top
of the seats

in front of them, dangling their whiffy trainers under the twins' noses.

"Get your smelly feet out of my face, bum-breath!" shouted Oliver.

"Who are you calling bum-breath, toad-face?" said Josh.

"I said, move your feet!" threatened Harry.

"What are you going to do about it?" said Jack.

"BOYS!" yelled Dad. "Don't make me come back there!"

Maisie Mae grunted as Harry shoved and poked at Jack's feet, which finally dropped to the floor. She fidgeted uncomfortably. Not only was she wedged

in between the gruesome twosome
with a holdall on her lap, but
there was something digging
into her bottom. She
wriggled and squirmed until she
could grab it.

"What is *this*?" she said, holding up
an extra-huge jar of Marmite.

"That's mine!" said Oliver. "What if
they don't have it in France? I can't go
a whole holiday without my morning
Marmite soldiers!" He snatched it from
her and held it tightly.

"Hey, that's *my* jar!" said Harry. "I
brought it so I can make my
famous Marmite pasta on the
campfire!" Maisie shuddered at
the thought. She was the only one
in her family who hated the icky sticky

brown stuff, and the rest of the boys had it with *everything*!

"Give it back!"

Harry dived across Maisie Mae and tried to grab the jar from Oliver, who pulled it back.

"I'll tell Mum!" screamed Maisie as the boys squabbled across her. They carried on grabbing and pushing until they both had a hold of the jar. "**MUU-UUM**!"

"Quiet down, back there!" Mum said, looking in the rear-view mirror.

"But the twins are fighting, and I'm caught in the middle!" squealed Maisie Mae.

"It's mine!" said Harry

"It's **MINE**!" shouted Ollie.

Just then, the lid **POPPED** off the jar and a huge dollop of

Marmite, warm from the heat of the car, oozed out on to Maisie's pink flowery T-shirt.

"**EEEWWWWW**!" shouted Maisie Mae. "You *Marmited* me!"

"Oh, for goodness' sake . . ." sighed Mum. "We'll pull in at the next service station. But after that, there's no stopping until we get on the ferry."

After a few miles, Dad pulled over and they all tumbled out, jumping around

and stretching their arms like they'd been caged up for months.

"Oh wait, here's *my* jar of Marmite!" said Harry, pulling an identical jar out from the car. "Fancy that!"

"**WHAT**?" barked Maisie Mae.

She glared at him until he backed away, holding up his hands, looking scared about what she might do next. "Woah there, sis!" he said, laughing nervously. "No harm done!"

Maisie started to run at the twins, who sped off across the car park.

"That's enough!" Mum caught Maisie by the arm and fished a new T-shirt out of the nearest suitcase, which Maisie changed into under a towel, just like she did when she was on the beach.

"France had better be worth it!" she said to herself, grumpily.

Mum took Arthur Stanley off to the toilets to do a much-needed nappy change, while the boys all zoomed off to the empty end of the car park with a ball, burning off some energy. Maisie smoothed out the creases in her clean top, listening to their shouts.

"**JACK ATTACK**!" yelled Jack, and Maisie Mae heard the scream as he bundled himself on to Josh.

"Five minutes, gang!" shouted Dad, coming back from the petrol station with a steaming hot cup of black coffee. It was so thick that when he tried to stir it, the little plastic stirrer snapped in two. Maisie stretched her legs and listened

to Dad muttering to himself. "This is
going to be the best holiday ever! Miles
and miles of French countryside for
the children to get lost in. *Completely*
lost . . ." he said with a
slightly manic
chuckle.

JACK
ATTACK!!

Maisie Mae walked about for a while, stretching her legs. She imagined that if she kept stretching and stretching them, one day she'd be really tall, maybe even as tall as Mum. She wandered over to a patch of mud by the side of the car park where Harry and Oliver were crouched down next to a wild-looking plant.

"I'm more French than *you*," sneered Oliver.

"No, I'm waaaaaay more French than you," Harry replied.

"*Pah!*" said Maisie Mae in her best accent. "I'm Frencher than the two of you put together!"

The boys turned around and then grinned at each other in a way that Maisie didn't like.

"Oh, really?" said Harry.

"Yup!" said Maisie Mae.

"Oh, *really*?" said Oliver.

"*Oui!*" she said, adding: "That means 'yup!' in French."

"OK, Maisie Mae," they said together. "**PROVE IT**!"

"**FINE**." Maisie crossed her arms. "I'll pass any test you set me." Just as Maisie was thinking up a way of proving how French she was, like eating a whole clove of garlic RAW, or counting to ten in French, the twins turned back around holding a squirmy, shiny, slimy, slithery **SNAIL**.

"Um, what's that?" she asked.

"Your lunch!" smiled Harry. "Didn't you know? French people eat snails *all the time*."

"Are you sure?" said Maisie Mae. The snail squirmed slowly in Harry's hand.

"You should know!" said Oliver. "If you really are the Frenchest of all, you should gobble it down like it was a Malteser!"

Maisie grabbed the snail between her thumb and finger, and stared at it. It looked back at her with its stalky eyes, and then curled up into its shell. She didn't like the idea of eating a poor, innocent snail, but she couldn't let the twins win!

"What's the matter, Maisie Mae? Lost your appetite?" taunted Oliver.

Maisie squinted at them and felt a rush of determination come over her.

I'll show them! she thought. She screwed her eyes shut and brought the snail up to her mouth.

"*Bon appetit!*" said Harry.

CHAPTER FOUR

Bonjour France!

"Maisie Mae!" shrieked Mum, running over and snatching the snail away from her mouth. She placed it carefully on a nearby leaf. "What on earth do you think you're doing?"

"Um . . . being French?" said Maisie Mae. Harry and Oliver were now lying on the floor, laughing like loons.

Lucky escape!

"I was hungry, so I thought I'd get some French food."

"You silly monkey!" said Mum. "French people *cook* snails before they eat them. And they certainly don't eat the shells!" She looked down at the twins, who were gasping for breath after laughing so much. "You two wouldn't have had anything to do with this, would you?"

"Us?" said Harry, trying his best to look offended. "Mother, how dare you!"

"Everyone. In the car. **NOW**!" Mum bellowed.

Mum pushed them across the car park and herded them into the car, strapping Arthur Stanley into his seat. "I don't want to hear a peep out of you lot until we're at the campsite, breathing fresh, clean, French air."

Maisie Mae settled down and read her book. Then she read another

one. And another one. Then they got on the ferry. Then she read a magazine. And another one. France was a loooooooong way away.

Finally, Maisie fell asleep and when she woke up, they were at the campsite. She eagerly looked around. It was dark. **SO** dark in fact that she couldn't see any of France, not even a tiny bit. She might as well have had a paper bag over her head.

"Where is it?" she asked.

"Where's what?" said Dad.

"France!"

"It's, um . . . out there. Somewhere. Let's all get our tents up and I'm sure it'll be there in the morning."

The boys all groaned.

"Did you get the brand-new ultra-cool pop-up tents?" said Josh.

"Nope!" said Mum. "We got the old second-hand pole and canvas tents that are actually *fun* to put up!"

The boys groaned again. Dad stood at the boot and dished out the tents. Josh and Jack had to share one and so did the twins, while Maisie had her very own zippy-uppy room in the **GIGANTIC** family-sized tent.

"Thanks, Dad!" said Ollie. "We won't

be needing these!" He pulled out the tent's instructions and crumpled them up into a ball. He threw them into the car and tipped all the poles and equipment out on to the ground. Dad and Mum set about putting up their tent, while Maisie handed them the right bits and played with a very grizzly Arthur Stanley. Jack and Josh hadn't even started on their tent.

Instead, they sat on a picnic blanket and ate chocolate that they had bought on the ferry.

"What's up boys? Not up to the challenge?" called Maisie Mae.

"Non-pop-up tents are stupid!" Josh called back.

"We're sleeping in the van!" said Jack.

"Suit yourselves! We'll be more

comfortable in the tents," said Dad tiredly. "And that's ours finished! Now, where are the sleeping bags?"

Even in the near-darkness, Maisie Mae could see her mum's face turn white.

"Sleeping bags?"

"You *did* pack the sleeping bags?" said Dad, his face dropping. "Didn't you?"

After a pause, Mum dashed to the van and began turning out all the bags on to the grass. She pulled out suitcase after suitcase, box after box until nothing was left.

"What are you looking for, Mum?" said Josh, laying back on something large and soft. Mum glared at him and marched over.

"**THESE**!" She whipped the soft things out from under him and Jack so

46

quickly that they tipped over on to the grass. They were the sleeping bags!

"Right, panic over," said Dad. "Go to sleep, everyone!"

Maisie gave Mum a kiss goodnight. "We are *definitely* in France, aren't we?" she asked.

"Of course we are, darling!" Mum laughed and gave her a hug. "You'll see – it'll all look better in the morning."

Maisie crawled into the tent, zipped her canvas door closed, and climbed gratefully into her sleeping bag. "Goodnight France," she muttered sleepily. "See you in the morning."

When Maisie Mae woke up she was immediately confused. Where was her super-comfy mattress? And her pretty princess duvet cover? And her perfectly PINK, extra **GIRLY, NO BOY ZONE** room?

"Muh? Where am I?" she mumbled. She saw

bright sunlight streaming through the coloured canvas and remembered, "Oh, that's right – **I'M IN FRANCE**!"

She leapt up, struggled with the zip to her room, and FELL into the tiny living area in the middle of the tent. She was *desperate* to get her first proper look at her first foreign country. She heard a sound like a warthog with the flu coming from the other room in the tent. Dad was snoring loudly. But Maisie Mae couldn't wait any longer for her parents to get up. She pulled on some wellies (her posh ones, with pink zebra print on them), unzipped the door and **FLUNG** herself outside.

BONJOUR
FRANCE!

"**BONJOUR FRANCE**!" she
shouted, throwing her arms wide and
taking a deep breath of French air. Then
she looked around.

♥ 50 ♥

She was standing in the middle of a large green field with lots of tents in it. Nearby was a field full of cows, along with a smell that reminded her of Harry and Oliver's dirty laundry bin. She could see a small building which probably had the toilets in it.

Everything looked . . . the same.

Nobody was even up, so she didn't even have anyone to talk to or practice her French on. Just then she heard footsteps behind her.

"*Bonjour, Mademoiselle!*"

Maisie Mae spun around, hoping to see a real, live **FRENCH PERSON**, but found the next best thing. It was Mum, with a big bag of **CROISSANTS** and **PAIN AU CHOCOLAT**!

"Ooh! Yummy! Are those just for us?" smiled Maisie.

"Hmm, that would be nice, wouldn't it? But I suppose we *should* wake the boys up and share them out," said Mum.

"Oh, I suppose," said Maisie Mae. "Bagsy I wake them!" She picked up a wooden spoon and a frying pan, and ran off to the twins' tent first. Carefully unzipping the door, she paused for a moment to watch them sleep, and then **BANGED** on the pan until the two boys sat bolt upright in their sleeping bags.

"Muh? Ninjas!" said Ollie sleepily.

"Run! The chickens are coming!" blurted Harry, his eyes still half-closed.

What were THEY dreaming about? thought Maisie.

"Breakfast, bozos!" she sang happily.

Then she tiptoed over to the minivan and let herself in the driver's seat. While Josh and Jack were snoozing in the back, she leant down on the horn and watched them **JUMP** up, instantly awake.

"Maisie!" complained Jack.

"Wakey wakey!" she said, and they all wandered over to Mum, who served their breakfast. The whole family, including a sleepy Dad, sat around in foldy-uppy chairs and munched on their still-fresh-from-the-baker's croissants.

"Mmm!" said Maisie Mae. "Thanks, Mum!"

After breakfast, the twins grabbed a football and ran off to play. Josh and Jack got their wash bags from the minivan.

"Just going to use the washrooms!" shouted Josh over to Mum and Dad.

"No *way*!" said Maisie Mae, looking at her brothers suspiciously. "You never wash at home! Being in a different country isn't going to make any difference!"

"Shut up, Muesli Mae," Jack called as he and Josh ran off.

Maisie Mae glared after them. *They are definitely up to something.*

As Mum tidied up and Dad changed Arthur Stanley's nappy, Maisie Mae walked slowly around their tents. She suddenly felt a bit lonely. If she was at home, she'd be over at Bethany-next-door's house already, probably making a Bratz TV show with Bethany's mum's camcorder. She wished she was there, and not all alone in a stupid field, *miles* away.

Just then, she saw a girl walking across the campsite. She was about

Maisie Mae's age, with short brown hair in a bob, and she wore a pair of **HUGE** pink sunglasses with sparkly diamante around the edges. She saw Maisie Mae looking over and smiled.

"*Bonjour,*" the girl said. *Wow!* thought Maisie Mae. *She's my age! She's glamorous! And she's really, properly, actually* **FRENCH**!

CHAPTER FIVE

French Best Friend

Maisie Mae gawped at the girl. She was soooooo glamorous! She walked over to meet her.

"Er, hi! I mean, *bonjour*," said Maisie.

"You are English! Welcome. You arrived last night, no?" said the girl. She spoke perfect English with a beautiful French accent.

"*Oui!* I'm Maisie Mae," said Maisie Mae, sticking out her hand to shake like Mum and Dad had taught her. The girl grabbed it and shook.

"Oh! Such a pretty name! I am Claudette," she said, and pulled Maisie towards her. She gave her a kiss on both cheeks like a proper French greeting!

"It will be so nice to have another girl around!

Would you like to come to the pool with me?"

"Yeah!" said Maisie Mae excitedly.

"There's a pool? Cool!" Harry and Ollie had appeared from nowhere, already muddy from messing around with a football.

"No! No way!" said Maisie Mae. "*I'm going to the pool, and I don't want smelly, muddy* **BOYS** *splashing about in it!*"

"You can't stop us!" said Oliver.

Maisie felt Mum's hand on her shoulder.

"Maisie Mae, the pool is there for everyone," Mum told her. "You can all have fun together."

They all grabbed their towels and costumes and sun cream.

"OK, but you can't walk with us!" said

Maisie. "You have to keep five paces behind at **ALL** times."

The boys rolled their eyes and hung back from the girls.

"Don't worry," said Claudette, leaning in close.

"My brother will be at the pool too, but we can stay in the shallow end to keep away from the boys."

"Absolutely!" said Maisie Mae. "How many brothers have you got?"

"Just one, but that is enough! I spend all my time trying to keep away from him. Boys are so – how do you say? – *stoopid*!" said Claudette, rolling her eyes.

Maisie Mae smiled. "Claudette," she

grinned. "I think you and I are going to get along *very* well!"

Maisie Mae got dressed into her swimming costume and met Claudette by the side of the pool. Claudette looked ultra-glam, wearing a pretty **PINK** swimming costume with a flowery pattern sewn into it.

"Claudette, you look so *chic*!" said Maisie. "Where's your brother?"

Claudette pointed to the deep end of the pool, where Harry and Oliver were already playing with a tall boy their own age who stood on the side.

"That's Laurent," she sighed. "Laurent! This is Maisie Mae!" she shouted. Laurent looked up and waved, but ducked as Harry and Ollie jumped into the pool with a SPLASH!

"**A-HAAAA! DIVE BOMB**!" shouted Harry, coming up for air.

To Maisie's surprise, Jack was already in the pool, burning off his energy by doing length after length after length. He and Josh must have known there was a pool and snuck off this morning to try and keep it to themselves!

"And that is my sister, Amelie," said Claudette, nodding

to the side of the pool, where a beautiful teenage girl lay sunbathing on a lounger. To her complete **HORROR**, Maisie saw Josh was next to her. He was talking to Claudette's sister with a strange, pathetic look on his face. To Maisie's surprise, rather than screaming and running away, Amelie was actually talking to him.

"You are sooooo lucky!" said Maisie Mae. "I'd completely **LOVE** to have a sister. Back home, I kind of *have*, but not really. I've got a friend, Bethany, who is my official best-friend-who-is-almost-as-good-as-a-sister."

They lowered themselves into the pool, which was already warm from the sun.

"Believe me, sisters are *just* as bad

as brothers!" said Claudette. "Amelie
is so . . . so . . . what is the word?
Autoritaire."

"What does that mean?" asked Maisie
Mae.

Claudette thought for a minute, then
started doing an impression of her
sister.

"Claudette!" she said in a high-
pitched voice. "You are so untidy! I
told you to pick up your clothes! Oh dear,
your hair is a mess!" Claudette
pretended to fuss with Maisie's
hair. Maisie Mae giggled.

"Ah! You mean 'bossy'!" she said.

"Yes! It's always, 'Hang up your
clothes, Claudette! Stand up
straight, Claudette! Learn your
lines, Claudette!'"

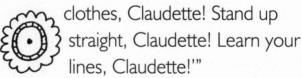

Maisie frowned. "Learn your lines?" she asked.

"Er, I mean, do my homework," she said, blushing. They looked over at Amelie, who was chatting with Josh and smiling a dazzling smile. "'Oh, look at me! I'm Amelie! I spend an hour in the shower every day! This is because I smell soooooo bad!'" said Claudette, making Maisie Mae giggle so much that she thought she was going to need to go and lie down.

Josh and Amelie shot them annoyed looks and got up, gathering up their things. Josh spoke in a loud voice so that Maisie Mae could hear them.

"Little sisters can be sooooo *annoying*, don't you think, Amelie?" he said, holding her towel for her. "Let's take a walk to get away from the **BABIES**!"

They walked off down the poolside, and Claudette leapt out and walked behind them, copying Amelie's walk and pout perfectly, until her big sister spun around, spouting a stream of angry French words before pushing her little sister in the pool. When

she bobbed back up to the surface,
Claudette was laughing harder than
ever, and Maisie found that she couldn't
stop either.

"This is going to be the best holiday
EVER!" she said, splashing Claudette
playfully.

CHAPTER SIX

Target in Sight

"Ah, *zut alors*! Not fair! That bounced!"

The next day, Maisie Mae and Claudette were involved in a completely **HECTIC** game of pool-ping-pong, a game they had invented by combining the only two activities that were available at the campsite – the swimming pool and the ping pong table. They had borrowed two bats and a ball from the games room (no one would miss them, as the ping-pong table had been put on its side and was being used to block a large hole in the wall), and were using the shallow end as their court. There weren't really any *rules*, you just had to keep the ball in the air for as long as possible. Maisie had found out though that it was **EXTRA** fun if you made the other player dive sideways for the ball, into the water.

"I don't think it *can* bounce, Claudette!" laughed Maisie Mae. She served again, and Claudette dived for the ball, causing a great big **SPLASH**!

"Careful girls!" said Mum. "Try not to splash the baby!" She was in the shallow end with Arthur Stanley, who wore a super-cool colourful mini wetsuit and a hat. He was screaming with delight as Mum dunked him in and out of the water. Every time she dipped him in, he'd chuckle and let out a stinky trump, which bubbled the water up like a Jacuzzi.

"Hey!" said Maisie Mae. "Arthur Stanley has got his own game – pool *pong*!"

Maisie Mae and Claudette put their bats down and leant against the side of the pool, soaking in the hot summer sun.

"We'll call it a draw," said Maisie Mae. She looked over at her friend, who wore a pretty pink ruffle-y swimming costume. "I love your cossie, Claudette! We should pretend to be mermaids!"

Claudette frowned at Maisie Mae as she tried to work out what she had just said.

"What is this thing, 'mermaid'?" she asked.

"Oh, sorry, it's . . . well it's like half a woman and half a fish. The fish end is the

See?

WEIRD.

bottom, not the head. That would be weird!" said Maisie Mae, but Claudette still looked puzzled. It turns out that a mermaid is a pretty hard thing to explain to someone who has no idea what you're going on about. Luckily at that moment, Laurent arrived with Jack, Harry and Oliver.

"Laurent?" called Claudette. "*Qu'est que c'est, une* 'mermaid'?"

Laurent looked puzzled too for a moment, but then clicked his finger and translated.

"*Sirene!*" he said, and Claudette seemed to understand. Well, she nodded and dived underneath the water. Maisie Mae would have joined her, but she had noticed something . . . something *suspicious*.

Harry and Oliver were standing behind Laurent with a familiar look on their faces. It was a kind of half-smirk that they did every time they were planning something. They did it the time that they booby-trapped the fridge to squirt cola at whoever tried to open the door. They did it the time that they told Dad they wanted help in the garden, and months later when the daffodils grew up in the flowerbed, they spelt out the word '**BUM**'. And they did it the time that they swapped the insides of their super-soldier talking toy with Maisie Mae's 'Speak and Play' Barbie doll, so that whenever she raised Barbie's arm, she'd shout '**ENEMY RIGHT AHEAD! FIRE AT WILL**!" in a deep, gruff voice.

"You're up to something," she said. She pulled herself out of the pool and stood with her arms folded, tapping her foot impatiently. Claudette stopped being a mermaid and joined her.

"Tell us."

"No chance, Queen of France!" said Harry. "Go back to your lame game."

"Tell us, or we get your mother over here!" said Claudette. Maisie Mae was impressed. She really *was* used to having annoying older brothers.

"You wouldn't dare!" said Jack.

Maisie Mae and Claudette looked at each other and smiled.

"**MUM**!" they called together. Mum looked up.

"All right!" said Oliver.

"What is it, darling?" said Mum, holding a smelly and soggy Arthur Stanley at arm's length.

"Nothing!" Maisie called back. She turned back to the twins. "OK, now spill the beans!"

Harry and Oliver reached into their

pockets and produced handfuls of empty water bombs. There were hundreds! Jack and Laurent suddenly appeared with a pair of **MASSIVE** water pistols. They were like bazookas!

"We're going to have a water fight!" said Jack.

"No, no!" corrected Laurent. "A water *war*!"

Maisie Mae and Claudette exchanged bored glances.

"Tsk! *Boys!*" said Claudette. Suddenly, a light bulb went off in Maisie Mae's head. A super-bright energy-saving one with the words 'Brilliant Idea' written on it. She grinned.

"I've got a better plan . . ."

"Target in sight," said Ollie. He crawled on his belly through some bushes over twigs and leaves. "Shhk! Water Wizard to Little Squirt! Do you receive me, over?"

"Of course I do, I'm right next to you," said Maisie Mae. "Why are you saying 'over'?"

"Shhk! It's what you say when you use a walkie-talkie. Over. Shhk!" Ollie whispered.

"But you haven't got a walkie-talkie!
You just keep making a 'Shhk!' noise
with your mouth." Maisie shook her
head impatiently. Claudette crawled into
position beside her.

"Whatever!" said Ollie. "Are the other
troops in position?"

Maisie parted some leaves in front of
her and peered out. Across the field, she
could just see the barrel of a super-soaker

poking out from behind the
toilet block. Laurent, Jack and
Harry were over there,
ready to pounce on the
target.

"Yep!" said Maisie
Mae.

"You're supposed
to say 'affirmative'!"
moaned Ollie.

"This is so exciting!"
squealed Claudette.

Maisie Mae looked
through the leaves
again, and could see
their target. Josh and
Amelie were sitting
on a picnic blanket half
way between them and the toilet block.

They were talking and gazing into each other's eyes with big soppy smiles. Maisie shuddered.

"Yuck! They're already so *wet* that they won't even notice a soaking!" she said, and Claudette giggled.

"Ready to attack, Little Squirt?" said Ollie.

Maisie elbowed him. "I'm not a squirt. You should call me 'Captain' or something," she demanded. "This was MY idea, after all!" Maisie parted the leaves again and saw Jack's head poking out from his hiding place. He gave a nod, and Maisie gave a thumbs-up back. "Weapons at the ready!"

She made sure Jack could see her hand as she counted down on her fingers.

Five . . .

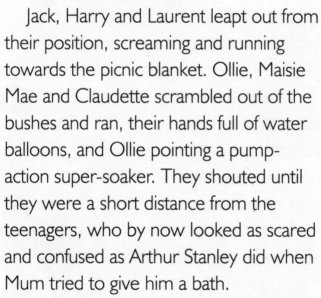

Four . . .

Three . . .

Two . . .

One!

"**ATTAAAAACK**!"

Jack, Harry and Laurent leapt out from their position, screaming and running towards the picnic blanket. Ollie, Maisie Mae and Claudette scrambled out of the bushes and ran, their hands full of water balloons, and Ollie pointing a pump-action super-soaker. They shouted until they were a short distance from the teenagers, who by now looked as scared and confused as Arthur Stanley did when Mum tried to give him a bath.

"What on earth . . . ?" Josh started to say.

"*Sacre bleu!*" said Amelie, standing up.

♥ 81 ♥

But neither of them got to finish their thoughts.

"**FIRE**!" shouted Maisie Mae, and they all hurled their water balloons and let rip with the water pistols at the same time. There was a flurry of water, balloons and water streams and the teenagers were drenched in water. You could hear Amelie's shouts from across the campsite. *In fact,* thought Maisie Mae, *Bethany-next-door could probably hear them over in America!*

"Aaaaaargh!" Amelie yelled. "You will pay for this!"

"I'm going to kill the lot of you until you are **DEAD**!" shouted Josh.

Maisie Mae and Claudette smiled and looked at their handiwork. Two soppy, wet, sopping wet teenagers stood dripping, while the rest of them exchanged high fives while running away.

"Who're the babies now, eh?" said Maisie Mae, running away and shrieking with laughter with Claudette.

CHAPTER SEVEN

Around the Campfire

"Teenagers are sooooo **YUCK**!" said Maisie Mae.

The whole family were gathered around a campfire with Claudette, Laurent and Amelie. This was excellent, as Maisie got to hang out with her new French best friend more, but on the other hand it also meant that Amelie got to sit with Josh. Maisie thought they would be mad about the water attack for a whole

MONTH, but they were so kissy-wissy and lovey-dovey that after they had shouted at their brothers and sisters, they just gazed into each other's eyes and started laughing like lovesick hyenas. They were all dried out now, and they were practically sitting on each other's laps.

"You can't annoy me, Maisie Mae!" said Josh. "I'm too busy having the best time of my life." He smiled and gazed at Amelie.

"Ugh! Vomit **CITY**!" said Maisie, and Claudette joined her in making sick noises. Mum passed them a huge bag of marshmallows.

"Here you go, girls," said Mum. "Take a wooden skewer and toast them on the campfire."

"Ah! My favourite!" said Claudette, turning to Maisie Mae. "Quick! Make sure we get **ALL** the pink ones!"

"That's what I was going to do!" said Maisie.

They quickly picked out as many **PINK** marshmallows from the bag as they could before Harry and Oliver wrestled the bag away from them.

"Laurent," said Harry. "You are one pretty cool French dude!"

"*Merci!*" said Laurent.

"**BUT**!" said Oliver, putting on his *this-is-my-deadly-serious* face. "How many marshmallows can *you* fit in your mouth?"

Everyone around the campfire laughed.

"What a stupid game!" said Amelie.

"Well," said Harry, "if you're saying that British people are better at marshmallow-stuffing than the French, then . . ."

"*Non, non, non,*" said Laurent. "I cannot have this. Prepare to lose, **LOSER**!"

Suddenly a daft campfire bet had grown into a **MAJOR** international competition, with Oliver playing for England and Laurent for France. Usually

Mum and Dad would tell them all to stop being so silly, but Dad ran back to the car to get more marshmallows! They all got behind their country and started chanting for them.

"Come on England!"

"Vive la France!"

They all clapped and cheered.

"**AND THE RESULTS**!" shouted Harry. "England managed twenty marshmallows, before he started to feel sick like a complete wimp—"

"**MMF**!" protested Ollie, his cheeks bulging out like a hungry hamster.

"And France managed . . . twenty! It's a draw!"

Ollie and Laurent shook hands and burst out laughing, spraying marshmallow all across the campfire.

"You lot seem to be having fun!" said a voice from behind them.

"Auntie Flo!" screamed Maisie Mae. They'd been so caught up in the craziness they hadn't even  noticed Auntie Flo and Uncle Jean-Paul arriving. "Hello, sweetiekins!" Auntie Flo swept Maisie up in a huge hug. Auntie Flo was *totally* her best ever auntie, maybe even best relative **EVER**. She lived in France with her French husband Jean-Paul, and she always looked completely fab. She had a long floaty, flowery skirt and a colourful blouse, topped with a gigantic floppy hat and so many bangles up her arm that she jangled when she walked. If they hadn't been making so much noise, they would have heard her coming a mile away!

"*Bonsoir*, Uncle Jean-Paul!" said Maisie Mae. "I've been practising my French. Listen: '*Je voudrais la robe rose!*'" She smiled. "Did I say it right?"

"Yes! Very good! 'I want the pink dress'. A very useful thing to say," said Uncle Jean-Paul. There were lots of greetings and big kisses on both cheeks, which Auntie Flo always did with an over-the-top '**MWAH MWAH**!' noise. "Tell me, Maisie Mae, who are your friends?"

Maisie grabbed Flo and Jean-Paul by the hands and led them around the campfire.

"The girl Josh is dribbling on is Amelie, the boy with the marshmallow down his T-shirt is Laurent, and this is my new French friend . . ." Maisie Mae looked around at where she had been sitting. There was no sign of Claudette anywhere! "Hmm. She was here a moment ago!"

"Who was, darling?" said Auntie Flo.

"My new friend, Claudette!" said Maisie Mae. She started looking around the campfire, and over at the tents, but Claudette was gone. "I didn't make her up, honest!"

"I'm sure you didn't, sweetie!" said Auntie Flo. "Now, who wants to help us put our tent up?"

Mum made Jack and the twins help out, and Laurent and Amelie said they had to go back to their tent as it was getting late. Amelie took **FOREVER** to say goodbye to Josh, even though she'd see him the very next day.

"Goodbye, my little English bunny!"
said Amelie. "Dream of me!"
"I'll miss you!" said Josh.

"**GROSS**!" said Maisie Mae.

While Dad put Arthur Stanley to bed and the others wrestled with the tent in the darkness, Maisie Mae sat in the light of the fire, thinking. Mum came over and gave her a cuddle.

"Are you OK, sweetheart? Missing home?" she said.

"A bit," nodded Maisie. "And it was so strange how Claudette disappeared. I keep thinking what I'd say to Bethany-next-door if she was here."

"Ah! I can help there!" said Mum, and she delved into a nearby bag. "Close your eyes."

Maisie Mae closed her eyes and felt something hard in her hands. She opened them and saw a book of postcards.

"They had lots at the campsite shop, but

I thought you'd like this one best. You can write to Bethany and tell her what you've been doing."

Maisie Mae smiled at the postcards. Each one had a tiny pink poodle looking **ADORABLE** in lots of different

photographs. She picked one where the poodle (she liked to think he'd be called Pepé) was wearing a beret. She clicked the top of her clicky pen and started to write:

Dear Bethany,

But she couldn't think of anything to write after that! She tried to think what she'd done; she'd met Claudette, gone to the pool, soaked Josh . . . She'd had a brilliant time so far, but nothing very French or **OOH LA LA** had happened. She thought of Bethany-next-door at Disney World, going on rides and meeting lots of famous people. She sighed and put the postcards away.

"*En guard!*" shouted Harry and Ollie

together. Maisie smiled and giggled as her daft brothers started sword-fighting with two sticks which were pink with bits of toasted marshmallow. Every time they hit each other, it left a large sticky mark on their T-shirts. Mum was laughing at them, even though they were getting filthy. Maisie Mae cuddled into Mum and smiled. Being in France might not be what she had expected, but it was still better than being at school!

CHAPTER EIGHT

On a Bike Ride

Maisie Mae stirred in her sleeping bag, waking to the sounds of Arthur Stanley cooing and gurgling happily in his travel cot. She had had a great night's sleep, going to bed with a tummy full of marshmallows. She had dreamt that she was a pretty **PINK** princess in a huge **PINK** tower, who had to be saved by a knight in shining PINK armour on a prancing PINK pony. She sat up, feeling a little bit sick and promising herself that she would never eat a pink marshmallow in her life again.

She crawled out of her tiny zipped-up room and climbed into some clothes. Mum was already outside, cooking breakfast.

"Good morning, princess!" she said, passing her a slice of hot buttered toast. "How did you sleep?"

"Pinkly," said Maisie Mae. She sleepily rubbed her eyes and munched slowly on her toast.

"Oh, that's good, isn't it?" said Mum. "Anyway, I hope you've got a lot of energy to burn, because I've found a place we can rent bikes! We're going on a ride!"

"Awesome!" came Jack's voice from his tent.

"Muu-uuum?" Maisie said in that way that meant she wanted something special. "Could Claudette come on our bike ride with us?"

"Hmm. I'm not sure, sweetie. She'd have to get permission from her mum and dad and hire her own bike . . ."

"Is that a 'yes'?" said Maisie Mae, making her eyes go wide and pulling her pouting puppy-dog face.

PUPPY DOG FACE

(always works...)

"Well . . ."

"Please?" said Maisie. "Pretty **PUR-LEEESE**?"

Mum paused, then smiled.

"OK then! Go and ask her," she said. "And make sure her mum agrees!"

Maisie Mae was already running across the campsite at her super-fast speed. Mum was shouting something but Maisie couldn't quite hear it. Something about being polite? She was *always* polite!

Maisie was halfway across the campsite when she realised that she had never been to Claudette's tent before and had no idea where she was going! She wandered about for a bit, until she heard the sound of singing nearby, which reminded her of Amelie, so she followed it. Maisie Mae turned a corner and was almost knocked on her bottom by what she saw.

It was definitely Claudette's tent (she could tell by the **PINK** wellies outside the door), but it wasn't like any tent that Maisie had ever seen before. A palace, yes, or a castle, maybe. But a tent? Maisie thought that it was so big it would have taken ten people to put it up! It was **AMAZING**. It was

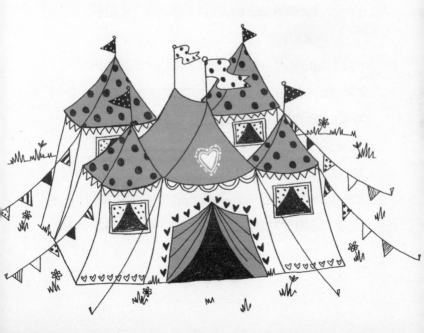

purple with a flag on the top and it didn't just have ropes pinning it to the ground – it had bunting! Lots of purple and pink flags fluttered down, keeping the tent upright. From what she could see, it had at least *four* rooms, each with its own little plastic windows and curtains.

Maisie stood gawping for a few moments, until Claudette popped her head out to put some shoes outside.

"Maisie Mae!" she called! "*Bonjour!* Have you come to have breakfast with us? I think I still have some marshmallows here . . ."

"Ugh! No, thank you. We're all going for a bike ride and you should come," said Maisie Mae, and then remembered what Mum had shouted about being polite. "I mean, please would you like to come out for a bike ride with us?"

"Oh, thank you!" said Claudette. "Who else will be coming?"

"Just me! Oh, and Mum. And Dad. And the baby," said Maisie Mae, thinking. "Oh, and my stinky brothers. But you can just ignore them."

Claudette looked very pleased to be asked, and gave Maisie Mae a **GIANT** hug. "OK, yes, I would love to!" she said.

"Cool!" said Maisie Mae. "But Mum said you have to get permission from your mum."

"Ah-ha!" said Claudette with a wink. "Leave that to me!"

She disappeared inside her castle-tent and Maisie Mae stood outside, gawping at how truly magnificent it was. It reminded her of the marquee that Dad had put in their garden for Auntie Flo's wedding, except there probably wasn't a dance floor in Claudette's tent. But then again . . .

Just then, she heard the sound of rapid-fire French being spoken by Claudette. Maisie Mae was amazed that anyone could talk that fast! She couldn't understand a word that was being said, of course, but Claudette was definitely speaking to her mum, and definitely getting her way. When the talking stopped, Claudette popped back out of the zippy door and smiled.

"It's fine! Mama's given me money for the bike, and enough for ice creams too!

Let's go!" she said. Maisie Mae held hands with her friend and they skipped all the way over to the bike-hire shop.

Maisie Mae's family was waiting at the shop, and Dad was practically holding on to the boys to stop them pouncing on the bikes they wanted, like they were hungry puppies in front of a sausage shop.

"OK, Maisie's here now. Go!" said Dad, and each boy **SCRAMBLED** to grab the bike they had had their eyes on. The twins quickly jumped on a pair of matching blue bikes, while Jack got a cool mountain bike with *forty* gears! Josh got one that was jet black, and Mum found a bike with a tiny seat on the back for Arthur Stanley. Dad got a red racer, which just left Maisie and Claudette to choose one each.

"Hmm . . . this one?" said Claudette, pointing to a silver and purple bike.

Maisie Mae shook her head. "No. It has to be just right," she said, scanning the hundreds of bikes in neat rows in the shop. Then she saw them. Two identical PINK bikes from the back of the shop, with shiny stickers, tassels on the handles and sparkly reflectors in the spokes.

"**SQUEEEEE**!" Maisie shrieked. "They're perfect!"

They happily hopped on them and joined the rest of the family.

"Everyone ready?" called Dad. "And we're off!"

They were soon zooming through the country lanes and past fields full of golden yellow wheat, huffing and puffing up hills and zooming down the other side. Maisie and Claudette kept glancing at each other and grinning. They were having a brilliant time, even though the twins were singing what felt like the bazillionth verse of 'Ten Green Bottles'.

"Village up ahead!" Dad called after a while. "Let's stop for a drink!"

Maisie Mae smiled at Claudette, who was just as puffed-out as she was. They all rolled into the car park of a café and parked their bikes. The twins and Jack got off and immediately started to chase each other around like they hadn't just cycled for a million miles!

Dad went to get ice creams and drinks and Mum turned and smiled as she saw a sleek car with two bikes strapped to the back pull into the car park.

"Great!" she said to Maisie Mae. "Auntie Flo and Uncle Jean-Paul have just arrived!"

Maisie Mae smiled too, but turned to see Claudette's face drop.

"What's the matter? It's just my auntie and uncle. You missed seeing them last night, but I'll introduce you. Uncle Jean-Paul is French too, so you'll have lots to talk about."

"Oh, that's OK! I don't need to meet them," said Claudette, looking red-faced, even though she had already caught her breath back.

Maisie Mae paused while Claudette started to act funny. She pulled out a pair of **HUGE** sunglasses, even though it wasn't that sunny anymore.

"Yoo-hoo!" called Auntie Flo from her car as she unstrapped her bike. "Hello, sweetiekins! Who's your little friend?"

Just then, Uncle Jean-Paul looked over at Maisie and Claudette and his mouth fell open in shock. He whispered over to Flo.

"What? Oh, don't be silly! It can't be!" said Auntie Flo, staring at the two girls. She gasped. "It *is*, isn't it?"

Maisie Mae hadn't felt so confused since Jack set her alarm clock for the middle of the night and she ended up getting dressed and setting off for school in the dark (she had only realised when she opened the door and saw an owl sitting on a lamp post). Auntie Flo and Uncle Jean-Paul walked over to them with looks of amazement on their faces.

"Hi Auntie Flo! This is—"

"Claudette?" said Uncle Jean-Paul.

"Oh. You know each other?" said Maisie Mae. Claudette looked down and went red again.

"*Bonjour*," she said shyly. Jean-Paul spoke to her in French, and they talked back and forth for a few moments until Maisie Mae couldn't stand it any longer.

"**WOAH**!" she said, and they all stopped talking. "**WHAT** is going on? Do you *know* Claudette?"

"Of course!" said Uncle Jean-Paul. "Everyone knows Claudette Renoir! She's the most famous child actress in France!"

CHAPTER NINE

Claudette's Secret

"You're a movie star?" said Maisie Mae.
"You have **GOT** to be kidding!"

Claudette was blushing underneath her huge sunglasses. She smiled at Maisie Mae, then nodded.

Maisie's mouth fell open in amazement. "You're *not* kidding?" said Maisie Mae. "Oh wow. Wowie! **WOWSER**! Claudette, why didn't you tell me?"

Claudette's cheeks were now the same shade of pink as her bike. She pulled Maisie away from Auntie Flo and Uncle Jean-Paul, who were still gawping.

"I am so, *so* sorry!" she began. "I did not want to lie to you, but I was having such a fun time! When I found out you were English, I thought that you would not know who I was, and I just wanted to have a normal holiday for once with my family. I did not want someone staring at me all the time like . . . well, like them." Claudette nodded towards Flo and Jean-Paul. "When I found out your relatives were French, I didn't want them to recognise me. That's why I disappeared when your Auntie Flo arrived at the campfire."

"So you're really an amazing movie star?" asked Maisie Mae.

"*Oui*," said Claudette. "Can you ever forgive me for not telling you?" she said, making the same puppy-dog eyes as Maisie did. Maisie Mae crossed her arms, looking Claudette up and down. Claudette gulped.

"Of course I can!" said Maisie Mae, throwing her arms around her friend.

"Finding out that my new friend is actually a super-mega-famous movie star is the best thing **EVER**!"

"You are not angry?" said Claudette.

"Of course I'm not!" said Maisie Mae. "What films have you been in? Tell me everything!"

"Everything? There are so many!" said Claudette, blushing. "There's *The Eiffel Tower Heist, Puppies in Paris, Sunshine in Calais…*"

"Woah! You're famous?" said Jack, butting in. "How famous? Do you know Thierry Henri?"

"Are you in real films, or lame *girlie* films?" asked Harry.

"Have you done any sword fighting?" said Oliver.

"All right everyone!" said Mum,

stepping in between the boys and a scared-looking Claudette. "Leave the poor girl alone! I'm sure Claudette just wants to have a normal holiday. On your bikes, you lot!"

The rest of the bike ride was uneventful, even though Uncle Jean-Paul kept swerving into the road by mistake because he was too busy staring at Claudette in amazement.

When they got back to the campsite, Claudette took Maisie Mae back to meet her mum and dad properly in what Maisie liked to call the **AMAZO-TENT**. Claudette's mum was really cool, and walked around in long flowing dresses singing French jazz, while her dad read a French newspaper and lounged in the sun.

"Wow. Your family are sooooo amazing!" said Maisie Mae. She was lying on a pop-up hammock with Claudette, drinking fruity French smoothies through a curly-wurly straw. "It's been super-ace spending my holiday with you."

"Yes," said Claudette, a bit sadly. "It is such a shame that I have to go back to Paris tomorrow."

Then Claudette gasped so loudly
that Maisie thought that she'd spilt ice-
cold smoothie on herself. "But of
course! Maisie Mae! You should
come with me to Paris!"

"Whaaaaat?" said Maisie Mae. "To
Paris? Me? With you?"

"Of course, if you want to. It's just a
little film première . . ."

"**DOUBLE** Whaaaaat? **YOU'RE**
inviting ME to a film première?
Really? *Really?*" said Maisie Mae, her
eyes almost popping out
of her head. Claudette smiled.

"Of course, Maisie Mae. I
will tell everyone you are my
film-star friend from *Angleterre*!"

They both screamed with excitement
and rocked the hammock so hard that

they fell out on to the ground in a giggly mess.

"I have to ask my parents," Maisie said when she caught her breath. "Let's go now!"

Maisie rushed back to her tent, followed by Claudette and her mum, and barrelled straight into Maisie's dad.

"Claudette'sgoingtoafiiillmmpremmmie-ierereannnnnndshe'sinvitedmeeeeee!" Maisie squealed. "Canigo canigo canigo?"

Dad laughed. "Slow down, Maisie! I didn't understand a word of that!"

"What is it, Maisie Mae?" Mum asked.

Maisie took a deep breath and tried to speak slowly. "Film. Premiere. Invited. Meeeeee! Can I go? Canigo canigo

CANIGOCANIGOCANIGOCANIGO?!?
canigo!"
she added,
jumping up and down.

"It's just a little film in
Paris," Claudette's mum
explained. "And of course,
Mrs Mae, you should come
too, as Maisie's chaperone.
The car can drop you back 'ere
afterwards."

Mum's mouth dropped to
the floor in amazement and
thrust Arthur Stanley into Dad's arms. "A
big girlie day out in Paris? Definitely!" she
said, excitedly. "**SQUEEEEE**!"

I didn't know Mum could squee! thought
Maisie Mae.

"It's a good thing I packed one of your

fancy pink dresses in case we decided to go somewhere posh for dinner," said Mum. "We're going to have a wonderful time, sweetheart!"

"I **KNOW**!" said Maisie Mae.

"Um . . ." said Dad, holding a wriggling Arthur Stanley. "I'll just stay here with the boys then, shall I?"

The next morning, Maisie took her dress and ran over to Claudette's tent, careful not to go near any puddles or patches of mud. It was still early morning and not many people were up yet, but Claudette had said to get to her tent as soon as possible. When Maisie arrived, Claudette was already up and having her hair done by a professional hairdresser.

"Good morning, Maisie!" she smiled. "Are you excited?"

"You bet!" said Maisie Mae. "I haven't been this excited since my auntie's wedding!" Maisie got dressed in one of Claudette's tent's many rooms, and came back out with a twirl, and everyone applauded. Claudette's hairdresser smiled, but muttered something in French.

"She would like to do your hair," translated Claudette.

"OK," said Maisie. "*Good luck!*"

Maisie Mae's curly hair was *impossible*.

More than one hairdresser had ended up in tears while they tried to untangle it. Claudette's hairdresser looked at her hairbrush, then shook her head. She went to her special bag and pulled out a *giant* brush and started to attack Maisie's mane. She had only managed a few tugs when the massive hairbrush **SNAPPED** in two! After more muttering, she patted Maisie's curls and placed a pretty pink headband on her head.

"*Voilà!*" said the hairdresser, with a shrug.

They heard a loud **BEEP** from outside the tent.

"Ah! That will be the car!" said Claudette's mum. "Everybody ready?"

Maisie Mae slipped on her shiny pink shoes and Claudette took her arm. They walked out of the tent, chatting about how far they had to go and how excited they were. But when Maisie saw the car she stopped dead.

"**OH**! **MY**! **GOODNESS**!" said Maisie Mae, as her mouth fell open and her heart went crazy. All her dreams had come true at once.

In front of them wasn't a car. It wasn't even a taxi, or a minibus or a coach.

It was a **SHINY. PINK.**

LIMOUSINE!

Maisie Mae could barely speak for once. She stood dumbly with a smile on her face as her mum took pictures of her and Claudette against the car.

Then the chauffeur opened the door with a little bow. "Mademoiselle Claudette, Mademoiselle Maisie," he smiled as they got inside. Maisie looked around the **HUGE** car as she sat down on the cosiest seats she had ever sat on. There was a sparkly disco ball, and a real fridge with bottles of lemonade and cola just for them.

Claudette's mum and Maisie's mum climbed in next to them and poured some fizzy wine into posh glasses.

"Can we do one thing before we leave the campsite?" Maisie Mae asked.

"But of course, what is it?" said Claudette's mum.

The driver pulled the limousine around to Maisie Mae's tent, and sounded the horn. Maisie pulled the window down and leant out see Harry

and Oliver playing keepy-uppy. They let
the ball drop to the floor as they stared
at her with open mouths. She laughed
as they gaped at her, and the limousine
pulled away.

"See you later, boys!" said Maisie Mae.

"Maisie?" Oliver said in amazement.

"Wrong." Maisie grinned. "I'm *Mademoiselle Maisie*, and I'm a **SUPERSTAR**!"

CHAPTER TEN

Red Carpet

Maisie Mae couldn't resist jumping up and down on the comfy seats, and Claudette joined in too.

"Wow! These seats are so springy we could bounce all the way to Paris!"

"Settle down, girls," said Mum. "We've got a long drive. Why don't you just look out of the window at the scenery for a while."

Maisie Mae bounced off the seat and landed on the floor with an "Ooof!"

"Mum, we're not even out of the campsite yet!" she said, crawling over to the window and pressing a button so it went down with a cool **ZZZZZZZ** sound. She looked out and let out a gasp. "Claudette, quick!"

Outside, Josh and Amelie were standing in the shade of a tree, holding hands and staring soppily into each other's eyes. They turned as the limousine drove past, and leapt apart when they heard their little sisters singing from the sunroof.

"Josh and Amelie, sitting in a tree! **K-I-S-S-I-N-G***!"*

The girls collapsed back into the car in a fit of giggles.

"Did you see Josh? He went as pink as this car!"

Maisie and Claudette giggled as the

huge car sped
along. They
looked out of the
window, practised
their film star smiles,
and they were just
playing noughts

and crosses (but using hearts and kisses instead) when Maisie saw something impossibly huge go past the window.

"Was that what I thought it was?" she said, rushing to the window. She pressed the button for it to go down, and immediately screamed with delight. "It is! It is! Mum, it's the Trifle Tower!"

Mum laughed. "The *Eiffel* Tower, sweetie. Do we have time to stop for a photo?"

"But of course! We have plenty of

time!" said Claudette's mum. She said something in French to the driver and the car slowed to a stop. The driver opened the door for them and they tumbled out on to the pavement. The two girls ran up to a bench and posed while Mum snapped away with their camera.

There were lots of tourists around doing the same thing, but as Maisie Mae was holding hands with Claudette and pretending to stretch up to try and reach the top of the tower, she noticed some people taking pictures of them. The driver tapped his watch, and Claudette's mum called them back to the limousine. As they walked back, some people pointed and Claudette smiled politely at them.

They got back in the limousine and drove off.

"The première is just around the corner," said Claudette's mum. Maisie Mae whispered to Claudette.

"Claudette, just *how* famous are you?"

Claudette shrugged. "Pretty famous, I guess."

As it turned out, Maisie Mae didn't

need to ask, as they turned a corner
and suddenly all she could see was

Claudette's face. They
were surrounded by
billboards and huge
posters of Claudette
smiling down at them!

"*Pretty* famous?" said
Maisie Mae. "More
like pretty amazingly
MEGA-famous!"

They stepped out on to
the red carpet and Maisie
Mae felt her heart jump
as she saw the lines
of photographers, all
shouting for them.
Claudette stepped
out first, and Maisie

waited for a second, feeling a bit nervous. But then Claudette's hand grabbed hers and pulled her out into the light.

Flashbulbs went off everywhere like it was a fireworks display! Suddenly everyone was shouting for Claudette. Maisie Mae stood straight, hardly moving. Claudette squeezed her hand and whispered in her ear.

"Do what I do. Have fun!" she smiled, and turned to the photographers. She said something to them in French, and Maisie Mae was sure that she heard her name in there somewhere. Suddenly, all the photographers were shouting for her too!

"Mademoiselle Mae! *Ici! Ici!*"

"This way, Maisie! Big smile!"

"Turn around!"

Maisie
and Claudette
smiled and danced and
jumped up and down with each
other, just like they were acting silly for
Mum's camera, and not the cameras of
the world's newspapers. They blew kisses
and twirled around on the spot, showing
off their pretty pink dresses. Maisie Mae
had never felt so amazing! Being friends
with Claudette practically made her a real
movie star too!

They got into the cinema and Maisie
Mae sat down with her new friend to
watch the movie, with her mum on
the other side of her. When the movie
started, it was all in French, so she
couldn't understand a word! It didn't
matter though, as she was having sooooo
much fun with her friend. She clapped
every time Claudette appeared in the
movie, making Claudette giggle.

"Claudette," whispered Maisie Mae.
"This is so *totally* awesome! And you're
a great actress!" Claudette squeezed her
hand in the dark.

"And you are a great friend!"
Claudette whispered back.
"Thank you for a super
holiday!"

Maisie stared at her friend up on the big screen and grinned. Suddenly she knew just what to put in her postcard to Bethany-next-door.

Dear Bethany

France is AMAZING! The sun shines everyday. We've had a great time and even been to a world movie premiere! The boys are _tres_ annoying as usual but I'v found a new French friend to pla with (don't worry! You're still m best-friend-who-is-almost-as-g -as-a-sister!) It turns out tha France is very OOH LA LA afte all! Love and hugs

Maisie Mae xx

…ethany-next-door

Next Door

(to Maisie's house)

ENGLAND

Join Maisie Mae's

NO BOYS ALLOWED CLUB

Sign up at www.lbkids.co.uk/noboysallowed
for free books, competition prizes,
news and more!

READ MORE FROM MAISIE MAE!

ISBN 978-0-349-00153-1

ISBN 978-0-349-00154-8

LISTEN TO THE MAISIE MAE AUDIOBOOKS

WIN a European camping holiday worth £1,000 with

By Wyndham Vacation Rentals

Fancy going on an amazing camping adventure, just like Maisie Mae? We've teamed up with Canvas Holidays to offer you the chance to win a fun-packed family holiday.

PLUS Get £100 off European camping breaks in 2015.

To enter the competition and claim your discount, **visit www.lbkids.co.uk/oohlala**